# Willow's Wonders

To the Ellis girls,
I am so excited
for you to meet
Willow! Know
that you are
God's girl!

# Willow's Wonders

TgosketchPress
Chicago, Illinois
www.tgosketch.com

ISBN-9781730855412

THIS BOOK IS DEDICATED TO EVERY GIRL
THAT FEELS SHE'S
DIFFERENT FROM ALL THE OTHERS.

I DON'T WANT TO BE HERE, WILLOW THOUGHT AS SHE TRUDGED UP THE STAIRS. SHE FELT AS IF EVERYONE WAS STARING AT HER, BUT WITHOUT HESITATION, SHE KEPT WALKING.

IT WAS WILLOW'S FIRST DAY AT HER NEW SCHOOL. SHE WASN'T TOO EXCITED ABOUT MOVING AND LEAVING HER FRIENDS BEHIND AT PARKER ELEMENTARY.

SHE LOOKED UP AT THE DOOR... ROOM 402, IT READ. TAKING A DEEP BREATH, SHE WALKED INTO THE CLASSROOM. NOT-KNOWING WHAT TO DO, WILLOW STOOD NEAR THE DOOR.

"HI, YOU MUST BE WILLOW", SAID THE LADY STANDING NEAR THE BOARD. STARTLED, WILLOW LOOKED UP AT THE TALL, SLENDER LADY, WHO WAS SMILING AT HER.

SHE COULD FEEL HER HEARTBEAT SLOWING DOWN.
"YES, I AM"
WILLOW NERVOUSLY REPLIED AS SHE LOOKED BACK DOWN AT
THE FLOOR.

THE SECONDS IT TOOK TO WALK TO HER DESK SEEMED LIKE AN HOUR. WILLOW SLID QUIETLY INTO HER SEAT AND OPENED HER BOOK, PRETENDING TO READ.

WILLOW STAYED TO HERSELF AT LUNCH AND DURING RECESS TIME. SHE WATCHED THE OTHER CHILDREN PLAY TOGETHER AND STARTED TO FEEL LIKE NO ONE EVEN NOTICED HER.

SMILING AND WAVING FRANTICALLY, HER MOM WAS WAITING FOR HER AT THE BUS STOP.

"SO TELL ME ABOUT YOUR DAY. HOW WAS IT? .DID YOU MAKE ANY NEW FRIENDS?" Mom asked.

WILLOW STARED UP BLANKLY AT HER MOM ONLY SHAKING HER HEAD, "NO."

AS SHE TURNED FROM THE SINK, SHE NOTICED
WILLOW SITTING AT THE TABLE WITH A LOOK
OF DEFEAT.

WITH HER MOST TENDER VOICE, MOM WHISPERED SOFTLY TO WILLOW, "BABY GIRL, YOU ARE BEAUTIFUL IN EVERY WAY. WHEN GOD MADE YOU, HE TOOK HIS TIME TO MAKE SURE EVERYTHING WAS PERFECT."

MOM PUSHED BACK IN HER CHAIR AND EXTENDED HER HAND TO WILLOW. "COME WITH ME. I WANT TO SHOW YOU SOMETHING." WILLOW EXTENDED HER HAND AND WALKED DOWN THE HALLWAY WITH MOM.

MOM TURNED ON THE LIGHT IN THE BATHROOM AND WITH HER HANDS GRABBED WILLOW BY THE SHOULDERS AND STOOD HER IN FRONT OF THE MIRROR. WILLOW STARED BACK AT HERSELF WANTING TO CRY EVEN MORE.

"IF GOD MADE US TO ALL LOOK THE SAME, WE WOULDN'T APPRECIATE HIM FOR OUR OWN UNIQUENESS. HE MADE YOUR NOSE WIDE TO SMELL THE ARRAY OF FLOWERS HE CREATED. HE MADE YOUR HAIR THICK AND FLUFFY JUST LIKE JESUS WHO IS THE LAMB OF GOD. HE MADE YOUR SKIN THE COLOR OF SWEET CHOCOLATE BECAUSE HE KNEW YOU WOULD BE OH SO SWEET.

HE MADE YOU... YOU."

MOM SAID WITH A COMFORTING SMILE.

A SMILE BEGAN TO PEEK OUT OF THE CORNER OF WILLOWS' LIPS.

THAT NEXT MORNING, WILLOW SLOWLY WALKED TO THE STEPS OF THE BUS AND TOOK A DEEP BREATH.

AS SHE WENT NEAR THE BACK OF THE BUS, SHE HEARD THE MOST GENTLE VOICE. "YOU CAN SIT HERE." AS SHE TURNED TOWARD THE VOICE, SHE SAW A GIRL WITH TWO OF THE PRETTIEST PUFFS ON EACH SIDE OF HER HEAD SMILING AT HER.

## The Author

Nicalondria Kelley is a native Houstonian. She has been an educator for the past 11 years and has a passion for children. Children's literature is important to her, and she wants to write books to help children appreciate their differences gifted to them by God. She is married to Willie Kelley II and they have one son, Willie Kelley III.

## The Illustrating Team

Tyrus Goshay is the owner of Tgosketch Illustration. Tyrus is an award-winning digital illustrator and 3D artist with over 18 years of experience. He serves as a college professor, teaching both game design and illustration in his off time. Tyrus has a Bachelor's in Computer Animation and Multimedia and a Master's in Teaching With Technology (MALT). He has contributed to several award-winning projects in the world of toy design and has been recognized for his achievements in academia as well. He also has tutorials in illustration and digital sculpting available on the web. Special Thanks to my Assistant Artist Sawyer Cloud who did a fanstic job on this assignment and brought Willows' story to life!

Visit his bookstore, and see other books that he has illustrated.

www.tgosketch.com
www.facebook.com/Tgosketch
tgosketch@gmail.com
Instagram/tgosketch

50356720R00015

Made in the USA
Columbia, SC
05 February 2019